| Good things about being Fashion Kitty | Bad things about being Fashion Kitty |
|---|---|
| 1. Can help kitties in need, which is very important. | 1. Cannot change into Fashion Kitty at will. |
| 2. Get to fly in the sky, which is amazing. | 2. Can change into Fashion Kitty only when someone calls for help or is about to make a fashion faux pas. |
| 3. Get to wear super-hero outfit. | 3. Cannot tell anyone I am Fashion Kitty. |
| 4. Get to have name in the newspaper. | 4. Cannot share my adventures with anyone. |
| 5. Get to meet new kitties. | |

# Fashion Kitty

## versus

I have a fashion emergency!

# the **Fashion Queen**

## Charise Mericle Harper

Hyperion Paperbacks
for Children

New York

Text and illustrations copyright © 2007
by Charise Mericle Harper

For information address Hyperion Books for Children,
114 Fifth Avenue,
New York, New York 10011-5690.

Printed in Singapore

First Hyperion Paperback Edition
10 9 8 7 6 5 4 3 2
Library of Congress Cataloging-in-Publication Data on file.
ISBN-13: 978-0-7868-3726-7
ISBN-10: 0-7868-3726-8
Reinforced binding

Visit www.hyperionbooksforchildren.com

This is Kiki Kittie.

And this is Fashion Kitty, her secret identity.

Kiki Kittie mixes stripes, solids, patterns, and colors with style.

Lana is Kiki's little sister. Lana has her own fashion style.

Sometimes Kiki thinks that Lana is more annoying than other times, and this was definitely one of those "sometimes."

No! Cassandra did, silly! The Fashion Queen.

And the most amazing knower of fashion ever.

And then Lana skipped off so fast she didn't hear another word Kiki said.

It is not very satisfying to do lots of arguing first thing in the morning before breakfast.

And it is especially not
very satisfying to do
lots of arguing with a
four-year-old who
thinks she is always
right.

Kiki tried to smile and make herself feel better, but inside her head she was thinking about the two things she knew about Cassandra . . .

and the one thing she didn't know
but was probably going to find out.

It's not a good thing to decide you don't
like someone before you even meet them,
but it can happen.

And sometimes once you do meet them it only takes a few words to decide that yes, you were right, you do not like them even one little bit.

Kiki was mad on the outside, sad on the inside, and wishing for the one thing that was not going to happen.

It's not easy to keep a super power a secret.
Especially when you'd like to use it to help yourself.

By lunchtime the school was half full of
Cassandra clones,

and by three o'clock it was even worse.

Kiki could not believe that someone so new

could become popular so fast.

It was almost like magic.

It was like a kitty having a pet mouse. Or a kitty changing into a fashion superhero. It was unbelievable.

And everyone was talking about it.

Kiki went straight to her room . . .

and slammed the door!

Sometimes, when she is feeling blue, Kiki flips through her Fashion Kitty scrapbook. She has saved every mention Fashion Kitty has ever gotten in the local newspaper.

Kiki was still feeling a little depressed, which is a word that means sad, yucky, and blah all mixed together, when she heard a fashion distress call.

said Mother, Father, and Lana Kittie all at once when they saw her.

and she flew up into the sky.

The signal was strong, then weak, then strong, then weak again.

Sounds like someone is having trouble deciding what to wear.

Inside the house that is exactly what was happening.

Does this look OK?

I just can't decide.

Fashion Kitty flew down to the bedroom window and knocked on the glass.

Let me in! Open up! Let me in!

Oh, my gosh! It's you! Fashion Kitty!

And you're Sandy . . . one of Cassandra's new friends.

Oh, yes! Isn't she fabulous? Do you know her?

You're friends with her, aren't you?

Fashion Kitty had to explain the difference between "anti" (which means against) and "auntie" (which is someone who is related to you and hopefully gives you nice presents on your birthday).

Up until two days ago pink was my most favorite color in the whole world.

Uh-huh...

I'm wearing my only anti-color outfit!

Everything else in my closet is a little pink, sort of pink, mostly pink, or all pink!

Sandy held up a strange-looking shirt.

I'm coloring in the pink stripes with this black marker, but now the marker is running out of ink, and I'm not even finished! I have two whole stripes left.

Oh, my!

Did you bring some markers? Please say you did!

Fashion Kitty had never met anyone who talked as much as Sandy.

Fashion Kitty paused. Because a fashion hero should mostly try to be kind, even if it is not the easy thing to do.

Fashion Kitty waited, and Sandy waited, and Fashion Kitty waited, and Sandy waited.

Then Fashion Kitty remembered and said:

Um . . . I've finished talking.

Oh, Fashion Kitty! What a relief! Because I really do love pink!

Isn't pink the most wonderful color ever?

I'm going to wear Auntie Bernice's outfit tomorrow.

27

Fashion Kitty thought carefully
about what to say next.

Then Sandy threw
her black marker
out the window.

Luckily it landed right in a trash can,
because nobody likes a litterbug, even
a cute pink one.

When Kiki walked in the front door, Mother, Father, and Lana kittie said:

all at the same time.

Kiki liked to have some quiet time after a big Fashion Kitty adventure, so the family left her alone to eat her dinner. This was hard for Lana.

After dinner, Kiki went straight to bed.
She knew three things about tomorrow.

It's nice to be right, but somehow not that satisfying if you are right about something bad.

And then Cassandra and her mumbling kitty clones walked off.

But Kiki didn't feel much better, so she guessed that Sandy wasn't feeling much better, either. And she was right.

But as the day went on, Sandy realized she was not as alone as she thought she was. And something happened that surprised even Kiki.

It started with some thinking,

and then some talking,

and then some friendly support,

and finally some doing.

It was a movement in pink.

I'm wearing pink

to show

my support for Sandy

and Fashion Kitty!

Almost everyone joined in, even some of the boys.
This was a very brave fashion thing for a boy to
do, because pink is not a normal boy color.

It's daring, but I'm wearing this pink shirt.

I've got pink socks. I'm doing my part.

Kiki could not believe it.

June, can you believe this?

It's great!

She was overjoyed, which means, happy, happy, happy!

This is the most amazing thing that has ever happened at school.

Everyone is together.

Cassandra could not believe it, either.

I cannot believe this! I am in a sea of pink!

She was incensed, which means, mad, mad, mad!

It's all that stupid Fashion Kitty's fault!

She's ruined everything!

When you have the fashion popularity spotlight all to yourself,

it's not easy to give it up,

even if you don't deserve it anymore.

For days it seemed like all everyone could talk about was Fashion Kitty . . .

Fashion Kitty, and more Fashion Kitty.

Even Kiki was getting a little tired of it.

Fashion Kitty this! Fashion Kitty that! Can we please talk about something else?

Kiki!

Kiki Kittie! Shame on you! You're jealous of Fashion Kitty, aren't you?

No! I...

It's not easy to keep two big secrets from your best kitty friend in the whole world.

I can't eat lunch with you if you are going to be that way.

Kiki tried not to think about Mousie or Fashion Kitty

as she ate her lunch.

Not far away, someone else was wishing she didn't have to think about Fashion Kitty, either.

And that someone was stamping her foot on the ground, because that was what she did when she was really

## mad.

Cassandra imagined all the ways she could make Fashion Kitty look silly, and all the things she wished she could hear Fashion Kitty say. These imaginings made her smile a very wicked smile.

WICKED

NASTY

On the following pages, cut along the dotted lines. Mix and match what Cassandra is thinking.

MEAN

Oh, Cassandra,
wonderful Cassandra,
Queen of Fashion.

I am a prisoner
of my own fashion.
Forgive me.

I should be
locked in
fashion prison.

Oh, Cassandra, most beautiful kitty in the whole world.

I am a big fashion chicken. Bawk, Bawk!

I do not have any fashion sense, not even in one little toe.

Cassandra!
True one and only
Fashion Queen.

I am a
fashion baby.

I have two left
feet when it comes
to fashion.

She didn't know that Fashion Kitty (MOKA* kiki kittie) was already suffering, but not quite in the way Cassandra had imagined.

I wish you could be Fashion Kitty all the time.

Can't you change into Fashion Kitty now so we can play?

No.

How about for my birthday? Can you be Fashion Kitty on my birthday

Why aren't you wearing more pink? I thought Fashion Kitty loved pink.

Sandy says pink is Fashion Kitty's favorite color.

See! I'm wearing it for you. I mean her.

*MOKA
(most often known as)

This was almost too much Fashion Kitty, even for Kiki.

Fashion Kitty told Sandy that pink *was one of* her favorite colors! Not her *only* favorite color.

She likes other colors, too!

See! Fashion Kitty wouldn't yell at me like you do! That's why I like her.

Unfortunately, it did not end well.

Don't bother me!

KIKI'S ROOM

SLAM

Kiki just couldn't help it.

Mother and Father kittie looked at each other. They did not like to hear doors slamming shut.

But before Father kittie could say anything about the door, Mother kittie said:

Come here, Lana. Let's make some cookies together.

Sometimes mothers know the exact right thing to say and when to say it.

Lana ran to the kitchen, forgetting all about kiki.

Cookies? Yummy!

And Father kittie forgot about the slamming door.

I do love fresh-baked cookies!

Mother kittie could tell that kiki was having a hard time being a fashion hero, and it would not make things one bit better if she got in trouble for slamming her door.

Across town, Cassandra was up to no good.

Cassandra waited, waited, and waited,

*mistake

but still no Fashion Kitty.

She didn't know that Fashion Kitty could only respond to real fashion emergencies, and not a fake fashion faux pas.

That night two very different kitties went to sleep with smiles on their lips.

One kitty was right, and the other kitty was wrong. Very wrong!

The next morning, Kiki made a special effort to be nice to Lana,

I think these cookies you made last night are amazing!

You do?

and on the way to school she made a promise to herself.

I will make up with June, and talk about how great Fashion Kitty is, for as long as she wants.

She felt very good.

Very good until...

"But" was a big word for Kiki that day.

The One and Only *Fashion Almanack* is a fake! But I can't say how I know that.

Fashion Kitty did not visit Cassandra last night. But I can't say how I know that.

Cassandra wrote *The One and Only Fashion Almanack* herself. But I can't say how I know that.

By the end of the day she felt very angry.

On the way home from school, Kiki thought about all the things that bothered her.

Everyone thinks Fashion Kitty picked out bossy Cassandra to be a fashion messenger.

Everyone thinks Fashion Kitty gave Cassandra a special gift.

Everyone thinks that Fashion Kitty wrote a book filled with spelling mistakes. Nobody spells "almanac" with a "k" at the end.

But the thing that bothered her the most was:

It's not fair that
I can't change into
Fashion Kitty and tell
everyone the truth!

And really, if you thought about it,
she was right. It wasn't fair at all.

Cassandra was so happy she skipped all the way home.

Cassandra! You are such a genius!

I can't wait to add more pages to the Almanack.

I have fashion power!

And though she didn't look any different, Cassandra certainly seemed to be the Fashion Queen once again.

59

Did Fashion Kitty really write a fashion almond?

It's "fashion almanac," and no, she didn't.

I didn't think so, because if I wrote a whole book I'd be really happy and proud.

And you don't look like either of those things.

Kiki walked over to Lana and gave her a hug.

Sometimes Lana was much smarter than a normal four-year-old, and that was what made her special.

The next day, Cassandra was ready for everyone, with some new fashion rules.

Cassandra was using her fashion almanac to make everyone wear exactly what she wanted.
She was abusing her fashion power.

Sometimes when a kitty is desperate she might decide to do the wrong thing.

It wasn't a fashion emergency, but it was an emergency for the sake of fashion, and that was good enough.

Fashion Kitty flew as fast as she could, and she caught poor Carol Anne by surprise. She was so shocked she broke her necklace by accident.

Carol Anne, put the money back, and I'll meet you in your room.

Agghh!

Boo-hoo! Boo-hoo! I'm so sorry! I just didn't know what else to do.

I didn't want to break your fashion rules, but I don't have a black hat.

Shhhh, Carol Anne. Those aren't my rules. I didn't write that book.

You didn't? But Cassandra told everyone you did. She said you gave her the almanac.

I did not write that book. It's full of spelling mistakes and . . .

I'm a terrific speller!

It hurts me to say this, but Cassandra is dishonest.

She's a bad kitty!

So I don't have to wear a black hat tomorrow?

No, you don't!!

Both Carol Anne and Fashion Kitty felt a lot better.

Excuse me, Fashion Kitty.

You don't have to raise your hand.

Oh . . . but how is anyone going to believe me?

About meeting you and what you said.

Fashion Kitty thought about it while she fixed Carol Anne's favorite necklace.

And when it was time to go they had a plan all worked out.

One more twist and it's as good as new.

Thank you, Fashion Kitty!

Happy to help!

Fashion Kitty flew home, and she felt as light as an autumn leaf. She looked at all the twinkling lights below her, and even though the air was cold she didn't mind it one bit.

Lana was still up when Kiki walked in the door. She was full of questions.

Did you fight with Cassandra?

Did you beat her up?

Did she cry?

Well, I certainly hope there was no fighting.

Calm down, Lana.

said Mother Kittie, and then she looked at Kiki.

No. I wasn't in a fight . . .

But I'm pretty sure I won. . . .

I don't get it!

What happened?

The next day was a big day.  It started off as
a big black-hat day.

And then Cassandra spotted Carol Anne.

All the kitties gasped in horror.

Cassandra was happy that everyone was watching her. She was going to make an example out of Carol Anne. She was going to teach her a lesson.

Carol Anne looked nervous, but she took a deep breath and said:

I don't want Fashion Kitty to disappear.

But I would like to rip up that book.

The crowd of kitties started mumbling excitedly.

Uh . . . aha!

Cassandra was a little confused. What Carol Anne had said was not what she had expected.

If it had been the olden times she would have said:

Off with her head!

Take her to the dungeon!

Arrest her!

But you couldn't really do that kind of thing today, in a modern school yard. Cassandra couldn't think of what to say, so she said:

one more time while her kitty brain tried to think of something clever.

Everyone tried to get a peek at the cover to see if Carol Anne was right.

Cassandra tried to cover up the *k* with her paw.

You're just jealous! Jealous because Fashion Kitty came to visit me!

Yeah! You're a jealous kitty!

Now Carol Anne was feeling very brave.

Fashion Kitty didn't visit you!

I can prove it! She gave me this note.

Are you sure? Maybe you wrote that note yourself!

Maybe you're lying!

What Carol Anne said next shocked and excited everyone. It shocked Cassandra so much that she dropped the fashion almanac and ran all the way home.

Everyone wanted to see the photo, and everyone wanted to see the note. The principal put them both on display in the gym for the last two hours of school. They were all was too excited to work anyway.

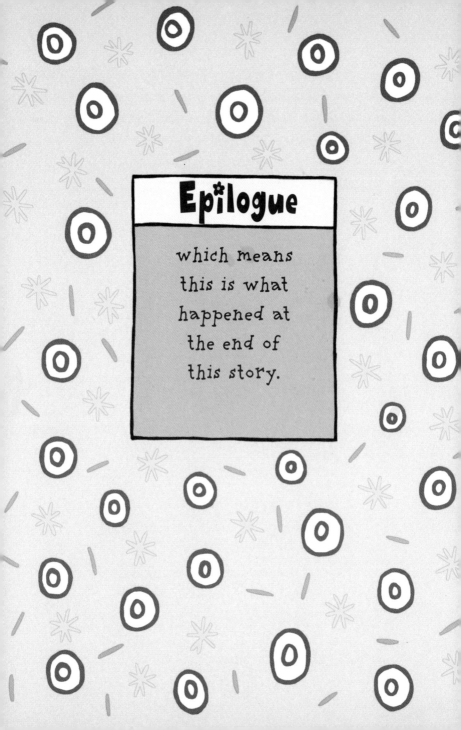

# Epilogue

which means
this is what
happened at
the end of
this story.

To show how angry they were with Cassandra, all of the students marched to her house and threw their black hats on her front lawn. It wasn't a nice thing to do, and it wasn't a supermean thing to do, but it was something to do with all the extra black hats that made sense.

The next day when Cassandra went back to school, she pretended like nothing had ever happened.

She was a fantastic actress. The drama teacher heard about her talent and soon had her busy rehearsing for the Thanksgiving play.

I'm just too busy to worry about fashion anymore.

I'm the princess turkey in the play.

I am the leader.

Come on, follow me, little turkeys.

She was perfect for the part.

Kiki and June were best friends again, and
Kiki was even making a special effort to be
nice to Lana.

Thought Kiki Kittie, and that was a very nice thing to be thinking right before falling asleep.

## NOTE:

I, Fashion Kitty, did not write The One and Only Fashion Almanack. (And please remember, there is no "k" on the end of the almanac.) FIGHT FOR FREE FASHION

*Fashion Kitty*

The End,
or is it . . . ?

Coming soon . . .

# Fashion Kitty
## and the
## Unlikely Hero